For Collette and the wee lads,
Russell and Ian—S. P.

For Lindsay, Luke, Lance,
and my mom—M. N.

Designed by Winnie Ho

Printed in the United States of America

First Edition

10 9 8 7 6 5 4 3 2

ISBN 978-1-4231-4361-1

F322-8368-0-12191

Visit www.disneybooks.com

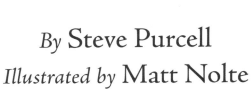

BRAVE
One Perfect Day

By Steve Purcell

Illustrated by Matt Nolte

DISNEY PRESS

New York

**I** am Merida,
Princess of DunBroch.

Mum says, "A typical princess
must behave like one. . . ."

"Always elegant, never rough-housing.

Always nibbling, never gobbling.

Always smiling, never chortling.

Always listening, never doodling."

Castle life is filled with lessons, fittings, and princess duties.

But once in a blue moon . . .

I have a day with nothing to do but be me!

Those days are the best. . . .

The Scottish wilds are my kingdom.
They are filled with mystery, beauty,
and adventure!

I go where
the wind steers me . . .

and I let the world reveal itself.

I do the things that
challenge me . . .

and make my heart skip a beat.

I dream of what I want to be.

I think about families . . .

and mums and daughters.

And I explore,
sometimes finding places I've never been.

I imagine how old our kingdom is.

And who might have come this way before.

Were they wee sprites?

Or lumbering giants?
Or did they look just like me?

I race the sunset all the way home.

And I bring along bits of my adventures to share.

I have mighty eagle feathers for my brothers,

tall tales for my dad, and . . .

"Merida!"

"Wait, I know!"

"A princess must behave like a princess.
It's true."

"Always curious,
always adventurous . . .

and **never, ever typical.**"